For Lois Linker —F. W.

To my grandchildren —H. M. S.

For my friend Gema and her big family —E. O.

Also illustrated by Elena Odriozola

The Opposite

Published by
PEACHTREE PUBLISHERS
1700 Chattahoochee Avenue
Atlanta, Georgia 30318-2112
www.peachtree-online.com

Text © 2008 by Ferida Wolff and Harriet May Savitz
Illustrations © 2008 by Elena Odriozola

ISBN 13: 978-1-56145-466-2 / ISBN 10: 1-56145-466-4

First published in Great Britain in 2008 by Andersen Press, Ltd.

Printed in Singapore
10 9 8 7 6 5 4 3 2 1
First Edition

Cataloging-in-Publication Data is available from the Library of Congress

The Story Blanket

Ferida Wolff • Harriet May Savitz
Illustrated by Elena Odriozola

PEACHTREE
ATLANTA

Deep in the snow-covered mountains
was the tiny village where Babba Zarrah
lived. The children loved to settle down
on Babba Zarrah's big old blanket to
listen to her stories.

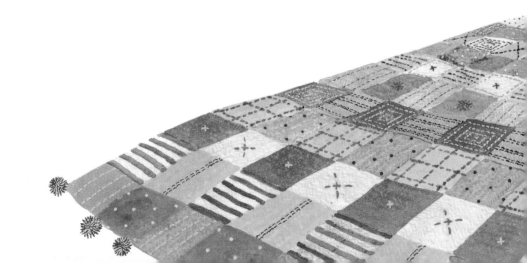

One day Babba Zarrah noticed there was a hole in Nikolai's shoe. When the children left, she decided to knit Nikolai some nice warm socks. But so much snow had fallen that winter that no one could get through to the village to deliver wool yarn. How could she knit warm socks without wool?

"Every question has an answer," said Babba Zarrah. "I just have to think of it."

She poured herself a glass of sweet tea to help her think. Before she had taken three sips, Babba Zarrah knew what to do.

"I will unravel a little of the story blanket and use the wool for Nikolai's socks!" she said.

Late at night, when everyone was asleep, Babba Zarrah trekked through the snow and left the socks on Nikolai's doorstep.

A few days later, Babba Zarrah noticed the postman looked quite chilly.

Soon after, the postman found a scarf wrapped around his mailbag when he left to start his morning rounds.

"Do you know who made it?" he asked everyone he met.

But no one did.

The schoolmaster was surprised to find a
pair of warm mittens on the woodpile when
he brought in wood for the school stove.

Mrs. Ivanov flapped the ravens from her
wash with the new knitted apron she
discovered beside her water pump.

Before long, the grocer
was wearing a new shawl instead
of her old moth-eaten one.

And the children had to sit closer
on the blanket when they came to
Babba Zarrah's for a story.

Day by day, the villagers grew more curious
about the mysterious gifts.

Baby Olga received a soft new blanket, and
the butcher showed off a fancy new woolen cap
that covered his shiny bald head.

The children were now squashed together
on Babba Zarrah's very small story blanket.

Confusion grew when the tailor's
scraggly cat showed up, purring and
grand, in a snug cat coat.

There was no story blanket left
to sit on.

The villagers asked the mayor to help them solve the mystery.

"You know what Babba Zarrah always says," the mayor replied. "Every question has an answer."

When the children saw the socks, the scarf, the mittens, the apron, the shawl, the cap, the baby blanket, and the cat coat all together, they shouted, "It looks like Babba Zarrah's old story blanket!"

"But she doesn't have it any more," said Nikolai.

"Aha!" said the mayor. "The mystery is solved. Babba Zarrah used the wool in her blanket to make these gifts. Now it's our turn to give Babba Zarrah a surprise."

So while Babba Zarrah slept, a few rows of wool were unraveled from every blanket in every household and left on Babba Zarrah's doorstep.

Babba Zarrah was amazed when she opened her front door in the morning. She had never seen so much wool yarn, in so many colors. And on top of it all was a sign that read:

For your
new story
blanket

The next time the children went to Babba Zarrah's for a story, there was a colorful new blanket to sit on and a tale about a village where everyone shared with each other.

As she hugged the children goodbye, Babba Zarrah noticed a hole in Alexandra's sweater. She wanted to knit Alexandra a surprise, but the snow was still on the hills and no wool yarn was to be had anywhere in the village.

Babba Zarrah knew that every question had an answer. She looked at her new story blanket and smiled.

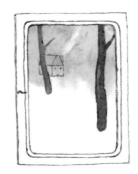